The Rice in the Pot Goes Round and Round

Written by **Wendy Wan-Long Shang**　　Illustrated by **Lorian Tu**

Orchard Books
New York
An Imprint of Scholastic Inc.

To my family, with love and gummi bears. — **W.W.S.**

For my grandfather Tu Bingyim who, legend has it,
hid a handful of rice in his mouth
for a week when he was a boy. — **L.T.**

When my family gets together we **laugh** and **sing,**

laugh and sing, laugh and sing.

When my family gets together we **laugh** and **sing**

At the table where my family gathers round.

The rice in the pot goes **round** and **round**,
round and **round**, **round** and **round**.

The rice in the pot goes **round** **and** **round**
At the table where my family gathers round.

Nai Nai drinks her tea with a **hoo,** hoo, hoo, hoo, hoo, hoo, **hoo,** hoo, hoo.

Nai Nai drinks her tea with a **hoo, hoo, hoo**
At the table where my family gathers round.

Ye Ye eats noodles going **slurp, slurp, slurp, slurp, slurp, slurp, slurp, slurp, slurp.**

Ye Ye eats noodles going **slurp, slurp, slurp**
At the table where my family gathers round.

Ma Ma picks a dumpling and **serves** one too,
serves one too, **serves** one too.

Ma Ma picks a dumpling and **serves one too**
At the table where my family gathers round.

Ba Ba takes a pancake to **roll up the duck,** **roll up the duck, roll up the duck,**

Ba Ba takes a pancake to **roll up the** duck
At the table where my family gathers round.

Ge Ge eats tofu with a **squish, squish, squish, squish, squish, squish, squish, squish, squish,**

Ge Ge eats tofu with a **squish, squish, squish**
At the table where my family gathers round.

Jie Jie holds chopsticks going **tap, tap, tap, tap, tap, tap, tap, tap, tap,**

Jie Jie holds chopsticks going **tap, tap, tap**
At the table where my family gathers round.

Di Di sucks an orange and says **yum, yum, yum, yum, yum, yum, yum, yum, yum,**

Di Di sucks an orange and says **yum, yum, yum**
At the table where my family gathers round.

When my family gets together it means **I love you,**

I love you, I love you.

When my family gets together it means **I love you**

At the table where my family gathers round.

Food Glossary

There are two major writing systems for Chinese, traditional and simplified. Traditional characters are the original form of the character, and have many strokes. Simplified characters employ fewer strokes to make them easier to use. Traditional characters here are written in red; simplified characters are in blue (if they are different from the traditional characters).

Rice is such an essential part of many Chinese meals that the word for rice can also mean "food."

飯 (饭) fàn

Tea is drunk throughout the meal, not just at the end.

茶 chá

Noodles, like rice, are an essential part of lots of Chinese cuisine. At special celebrations, like birthdays, noodles symbolize longevity or long life.

麵 (面) miàn

Dumplings have different types of filling, like meat, vegetables, or sweet bean paste, wrapped in dough. Jiǎozi are a popular kind of dumpling with ground pork in the middle.

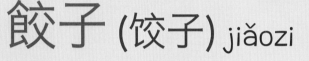

餃子 (饺子) jiǎozi

Peking duck is a very famous way to prepare duck. The skin is very crispy and flavorful. To enjoy Peking duck, diners wrap the meat and skin in a thin flour pancake, along with some vegetables and sauces.

北京烤鴨 (北京烤鸭) Běijīng kǎoyā

Tofu is made from soy milk. The curds of the soy milk are pressed into blocks, and can be soft or firm. The taste is very mild.

豆腐 dòufu

Fruit, like the **orange** in the book, is often served at the end of the meal.

橘子 júzi

A Chinese Family

The Chinese language has specific titles for all family members. What you call your grandfather on your mother's side is different from what you call your grandfather on your father's side. There are different names for siblings, too, depending on whether they are older or younger than you are.

Nǎinai (paternal grandmother)
rhymes with "bye-bye," with a slight inflection at the end 奶奶

Yéye (paternal grandfather)
pronounced with a short "e," as in "yet" without the "t" sound 爺爺 (爷爷)

Māma (mom)
pronounced with an "ah" sound 媽媽 (妈妈)

Bàba (dad)
pronounced with a short "ah" sound 爸爸

Gēge (older brother)
pronounced with a hard "g" and a short "uh" sound
as in "gull" (without the "l" sound) 哥哥

Jiějie (older sister)
the "ie" is pronounced as a "y" and a short "e"—the whole word
is pronounced "j-ye" with a slight inflection at the end 姐姐

Dìdi (younger brother)
rhymes with "Fifi" 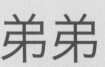 弟弟

Mèimei (younger sister)
sounds like "may may" 妹妹

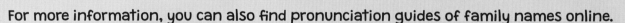

For more information, you can also find pronunciation guides of family names online.

Dining Etiquette

Every family and every culture has different rules for how to be polite at the dinner table. If you're enjoying a Chinese meal, here are some etiquette points to keep in mind:

- Sticking your chopsticks straight down into the rice is frowned upon. This is considered bad luck. (Also, do not use your chopsticks for playing or pointing!)

- If someone pours tea for you, you can say thank you, or tap the table with your index and middle fingers together if you're in the middle of a conversation or there's too much hubbub around the table.

- The grandfather in this story "slurps" his noodles. Some people think that making noises while you eat is rude, but other people would say he's enjoying them.

- While some cultures encourage you to clean your plate, at a Chinese table this could be interpreted as a sign that you haven't had enough to eat, and your host might urge you to eat more! Leave a little bit of food on your plate to show that you are full. (Your parents may feel differently, though.)

- Wherever you eat, acting with consideration for others is always a good idea. Be sure to say please and thank you, and show that you appreciate the food you receive and the people you are with.

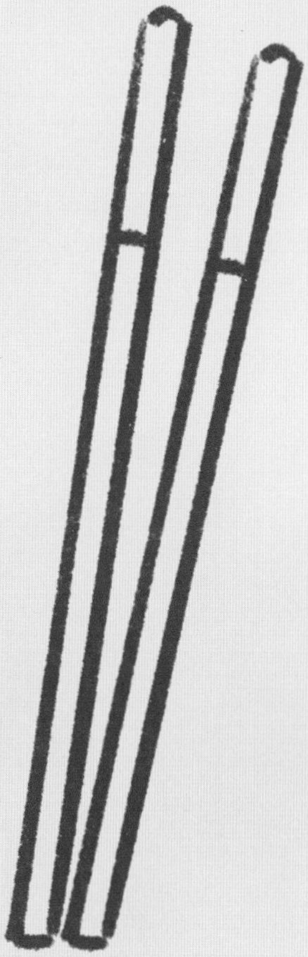

Author's Note

I have lots of memories of eating at round tables, usually at Chinese restaurants. One of the great things about a round table is that you can squeeze lots of people around it, and the lazy Susan in the middle means everyone has a chance to enjoy the dishes (and have some fun spinning the lazy Susan). The idea for this story came after celebrating Thanksgiving around a beautiful round rosewood table at my brother's house. While we drove home, the tune of "The Wheels on the Bus" started playing in my head and transformed into the book you hold now. I hope this book inspires YOU to make up your own song about the people and food you love.

Illustrator's Note

What is better than sharing a meal with loved ones? The sights, smells, sounds, tastes, and feels of such an experience are both heartwarming and unforgettable. The fondest memories I hold of my childhood are always paired with a delectable meal and have worked to shape me into the person I've grown up to be. I can still smell my grandmother's kitchen, hear the crackle of the oil in the wok, see the rainbow of veggies on the counter, and taste the sweet-savory cha siu bao, warm from the oven. We had a pot of rice that went round and round, and I remember my grandfather would always give my brother and me a bit extra. As an adult, I find a warm bowl of rice is my go-to comfort food. With that in mind, I created the illustrations for this book with the intent of conjuring a dream-like reminiscence — the kind that will hopefully transport you back to your own special memories of family and food.

Text copyright © 2021 by Wendy Wan-Long Shang · Illustrations copyright © 2021 by Lorian Tu · All rights reserved. Published by Orchard Books, an imprint of Scholastic Inc., *Publishers Since 1920*. ORCHARD BOOKS and design are registered trademarks of Watts Publishing Group, Ltd., used under license. SCHOLASTIC and associated logos are trademarks and/or registered trademarks of Scholastic Inc. The publisher does not have any control over and does not assume any responsibility for author or third-party websites or their content. · No part of this publication may be reproduced, stored in a retrieval system, or transmitted in any form or by any means, electronic, mechanical, photocopying, recording, or otherwise, without written permission of the publisher. For information regarding permission, write to Scholastic Inc., Attention: Permissions Department, 557 Broadway, New York, NY 10012. · This book is a work of fiction. Names, characters, places, and incidents are either the product of the author's imagination or are used fictitiously, and any resemblance to actual persons, living or dead, business establishments, events, or locales is entirely coincidental. · Library of Congress Cataloging-in-Publication Data available · ISBN 978-1-338-62119-8 · 10 9 8 7 6 5 4 3 2 1   21 22 23 24 25 · Printed in China   38
First edition, April 2021 · Book design by Rae Crawford · The text type was set in Grandstander Classic. The display type was set in Grandstander Classic Bold. · The illustrations were created using watercolor, gouache, colored pencil, and ink on hot press watercolor paper and edited Photoshop.